THIS BOOK BELONGS TO...

- - - - - - - - - - - - - - - - - - - -

- - - - - - - - - - - - - - - - - - - -

- - - - - - - - - - - - - - - - - - - -

To all those whose curiosity has led to amazing scientific discoveries – TH, LD.

Published in 2019 by Clink Street Publishing

Text copyright © Tanya Hutter and Lina Daniel 2019

Illustrations copyright © Karin Eklund 2019

Designed by Stefan Holliland

ISBN: Paperback 978-1-912850-38-9 ebook 978-1-912850-39-6

A CIP catalogue record for this book is available from the British Library.

About the book

The book is supported by the L'Oréal UK and Ireland For Women In Science Fellowship.

Disclaimer

The book aims to provide an introduction to basic concepts and has been simplified for the younger readers in the language, explanations and introduction of scientific facts. Some facts therefore are not fully accurate and do not accurately represent the timeline in which Darwin and other scientists discovered and contributed to the Theory of Evolution.

Written by Tanya Hutter & Lina Daniel

ANNA & EVAN
meet Charles
DARWIN

Illustrated by Karin Eklund

It is a sunny Sunday morning. Anna and Evan are very excited to spend a day at the local zoo.

They like animals very much and enjoy learning about them. They are curious about what they eat, where they live and how they behave.

"Look at the bears Anna!" said Evan.
"I wonder why they look so different?" asked Anna.

"One is brown, and one is white."

Anna grabbed Evan's hand and said, "Evan, close your eyes and whisper the magical words after me..."

"Excited to learn – eager to discover."

As they whisper the spell, a magical dust swirls around them, taking the children far into the sky and back in time.

Within seconds, Anna and Evan appear on a beach.
They see a huge ship, with white sails in the water.

Flamingo

Galapagos penguin

Marine iguana

Land iguana

Sally Lightfoot crab

Blue-footed booby

On the boat is written a name "BEAGLE".

They also notice many interesting animals
that they haven't seen before.

Sea lion

Saddleback
tortoise

Lava lizard

Suddenly a man approaches them and says, "Hello, I'm Charles Darwin."

North
America

Galapagos

South
America

"Hello Mr Darwin! My name is Anna and this is my brother Evan, nice to meet you," Anna replied.

"What are you doing here Mr Darwin?" Evan was very curious.
"I'm sailing around the world to discover and learn about different animals that live in different places," replies Darwin.

ope

Asia

Africa

Oceania

Antarctica

"Welcome to Galapagos Islands! It's a truly magical place!
It is made of many little islands, and it is home to animals
that don't live anywhere else on earth."

Birds

Reptiles

Insects

"So, what exactly have you been doing here?" asked both children, they still were confused. "I have been looking at different animals in the forests and jungles, in rivers and oceans, on mountains and even underground," Charles Darwin explained.

Amphibians

Sea creatures

Mammals

"I am collecting different types of plants, animals, rocks and fossils, because it is interesting to study how and why some are so similar to each other, and some of them are completely different," he continued.

"What are two young travellers like you doing here? Are you lost? How can I help?" asked Charles Darwin.

"Actually, we are looking for an explanation, maybe you would be able to help us. How come there are white coloured bears and brown coloured bears?"

"Ohhh that's a tricky question, but I think that I can offer an explanation.

Green warbler-finch: thin, probing beak for feeding on small insects

Large ground finch: large short beak for eating seeds

"Look around, can you see those birds? Can you spot the differences in their beaks? One has thin beak and he can eat small insects, the other has a large short beak to eat seeds. Isn't it interesting that they have different beaks to allow them to easily eat their favourite food?"

Saddle shaped shell

"That's interesting but still doesn't answer our question, why and how those changes occur?" Anna insists. "Patience my dear, listen carefully... I've noticed that animals at different places are better suited to living in that place," says Charles Darwin.

"For example, I saw two kinds of tortoises that live
on different islands. On one island, the leaves grow
higher above the ground, and the tortoises that live
there have long necks and a shell that allows them to
stretch high up to eat the leaves. On another island,
there are plenty of leaves that grow close to the ground,
and the tortoises that live there have short necks."

Dome shaped shell

"Such differences can be found all over the world with different types of animals."

African elephant

Asian elephant

"African elephants have large ears to help them cool down because Africa is so hot. The larger the area of the ear, the more heat can come out. Asian elephants live in a cool jungle and have small ears."

Arctic fox in the winter

"Another example is the Arctic fox - over the winter the arctic fox has a thick white fur, which helps it to stay warm and to camouflage itself in the snow."

Arctic fox in the summer

"But in spring,
the fur changes to a thinner,
brown-coloured fur."

Anna and Evan look at each other -

"We got it, thank you Mr Darwin!"

"I need to get back to my work now, safe travels kids!" said Charles Darwin. Anna and Evan hold hands and together they whisper the magical words...

"New things we learned, now it's time to be returned."

They appear back in the zoo.

"I know the answer!" Anna shouted excitedly.

"The colour of the bears' fur had changed in order to adapt themselves to their environment. The polar bear that lives in very cold places, has a thick white fur so he can stay warm and blend with the snow."

Anna and Evan felt pleased with what they learned, but it was time to go home.

At home, they showed their mother drawings
and maps from their special journey.

Anna and Evan are looking forward to
another learning adventure in the future.

Short biography

Charles Robert Darwin (1809–1882)

Charles was born in England in 1809.

Since he was a little boy, he was curious about nature and he spent much of his time outdoors looking at plants, flowers, insects and birds. His parents wanted him to become a medical doctor, but Charles prefered to become a minister in a church.

At 22 years old, he was unexpectedly invited to travel around the world with a captain of the Royal Navy named Robert FitzRoy. Charles decided to go. And so, in 1831, he began a 5-year sailing journey around the world on a ship called *HMS Beagle*. Charles was seasick while sailing, but luckily the boat stopped in many different places, allowing him to explore the land.

In 1835, he arrived at the Galapagos Islands, where he saw many animal species that don't live anywhere else on Earth. Throughout the voyage, he collected fossils, plants and animals from different places, and kept a diary describing everything he saw.

The *Beagle* returned to England in 1836, and Charles became a scientist. Together with other scientists, he studied the fossils, birds and plants he had collected during the voyage. He was also working on a theory to explain how creatures could change over time.

23 years later, in 1859, he published his famous book *'On the Origin of Species by Means of Natural Selection'*, which is considered one of the most important books on science ever written.

He died at the age of 73 and is buried in Westminster Abbey.

Dictionary

Environment – everything that surrounds a living thing.

Habitat – the place where an animal lives.

Species – a group of similar plants or animals that can produce an offspring.

Adaptation – a feature or behaviour that helps an animal survive in its environment.

Camouflage – a colour or shape in an animal's body that helps it blend into its environment.

Galapagos Islands – the islands lie in the Pacific Ocean and consist of 13 big islands and many small islands. The word Galapagos means "tortoises" in Spanish.

Fossils – impressions or preserved remains of animals or plants from a long time ago.

Biography – also called Bio, is a description of a person's life.

CPSIA information can be obtained
at www.ICGtesting.com
Printed in the USA
BVHW021010120219
540008BV00012B/52/P

* 9 7 8 1 9 1 2 8 5 0 3 8 9 *